Wizard or Witch?

A Magical World Awaits You
Read

THE SECRETS OF DROON

Wizard or Witch?

by Tony Abbott

Illustrated by David Merrell

Cover illustration by Tim Jessell

A
LITTLE APPLE
PAPERBACK

SCHOLASTIC INC.
New York Toronto London Auckland Sydney
Mexico City New Delhi Hong Kong Buenos Aires

No part of this publication may be reproduced in whole or in part, or stored in a retrieval system, or transmitted in any form or by any means, electronic, mechanical, photocopying, recording, or otherwise, without written permission of the publisher.
For information regarding permission, write to Scholastic Inc., Attention: Permissions Department, 557 Broadway, New York, NY 10012.

ISBN 0-439-56049-7

12 11 10 9 8 7 6 5 4   4 5 6 7 8 9/0

Printed in the U.S.A.   40
First printing, January 2004

For Janie and Lucy,
my amazing and magical daughters

Contents

Wizard or Witch?

One

This Magic Moment

It was the sound of words that woke me.

At first, they seemed strange and beautiful, like mysterious fish weaving around a swimmer.

Then the shouts came, and the running of feet, and the voices, full of fear, calling me. . . .

No. Wait. That's not right.

I need to begin this story properly.

It isn't every day a person gets to write in her Wizardbook. This is far too important to get wrong. The story I set down on these pages — every single word of it — has to be right.

It has to be perfect.

Perfect? Yes. That's part of the story, too.

Okay, then.

My name is Keeah. I live in Jaffa City, the royal capital of the land of Droon. King Zello is Droon's ruler and the leader of its people. He's also my father.

Queen Relna is my very beautiful and kind mother. She's a wizard of incredible power.

Since I'm their daughter, I'm a princess.

And a wizard.

The more I practice all my charms and spells — and the bright blue wizard sparks shooting from my fingertips have been getting stronger each day — the better it is for Droon.

That's because not all of Droon is good.

And *that*'s because of Lord Sparr.

I shiver even writing his name in my Wizardbook. Sparr is a sorcerer of great power. He wants to control not only his Dark Lands — the smelly, smoke-filled countries east of Jaffa City — but every single inch of Droon itself.

And not just Droon, either.

A long time ago, Sparr created the Three Powers — the Red Eye of Dawn, the Golden Wasp, and the Coiled Viper.

For ages and ages, these magical objects were lost.

Then, Sparr found his Powers — one after the other — until only the Red Eye remained hidden from him.

Of course, my parents and I aren't

the only ones trying to stop Sparr from ruling Droon.

The great wizard, Galen Longbeard, has fought the sorcerer and his army of Ninns forever, trying to keep them from taking over.

Or, he used to.

A very mysterious genie named Anusa took the wizard away from us on a long journey. Where Galen is now and when his quest will end, nobody really knows.

But Max, his trusty spider troll friend, is here to help us, along with many friendly people and creatures in every corner of Droon. They're part of this story, too.

Best of all are my friends Eric Hinkle, Julie Rubin, and Neal Kroger.

Ever since they discovered a magical staircase between us and the Upper World where they live, they've been helping me keep Droon safe.

Eric has even become a wizard with his own really strong magic. Julie now has the ability to fly. And Neal . . . well, Neal is Neal.

Droon can be pretty dangerous, but my friends are always here when I need them most.

I needed them today.

Which brings me to the beginning. I'll start my story with the very first thing I remember.

Morning . . .

The sun was just below the eastern hills. I was in my royal bed, asleep and dreaming . . . dreaming . . . dreaming . . . deep dreams. . . .

Krooth-ka . . . meshti . . . pah-la . . . Neffu!

"What?" I bolted up in bed thinking that someone had called out to me. Strange words I'd never heard before swam in my head for a moment, then faded.

Looking around, I saw hazy pink light beginning to streak the floor of my room.

"Who's there?" I said. "Mother? Father —"

Thump! Thump! The sound of running feet filled the corridors of the palace.

"Stop, you! Stop!" someone yelled.

Pushing aside the book lying next to me, I jumped up from my bed, only to find that I had fallen asleep in my clothes — blue tunic, leggings, and belt. My gold crown lay resting on my pillow. I put it on.

"Max? Max!" I called. He didn't answer. His tiny bed was all rumpled and empty in the corner.

A sudden cry came through the halls.

"It is mine . . . *mine!*"

A chill ran through me. The voice, part

hissing, part snarling, sounded like *his*. It sounded like the voice of Lord Sparr.

"Him? Here? Never!" I whispered.

Long ago, Galen had cast a spell against Sparr. He could never enter Jaffa City unless he was invited in. *And he never would be.*

I looked up at the ceiling. Objects I had levitated the night before — two clocks, a bucket, five pencils — still hung where I'd charmed them. Levitating things was my latest skill. Among the hovering objects was a glass ball that I always use to call my friends.

"Princess!" cried a fearful voice from below. It came from my parents' throne room.

"Coming!" I shouted. I glanced back at the floating ball. "Sorry, friends, I'll call you later. Right now, I'm needed!"

I knew going over the rooftops would

be even quicker than running through the palace halls, which I wasn't supposed to do anyway. So, I flung open the far door and dashed onto the stones of my balcony.

Above me, the sky was turning from deep violet to the pink of morning. The sun just peeped over the eastern horizon. I breathed it all in.

"Okay, Keeah," I said to myself. "It's magic time. Mother, Father, here I come!"

Trembling, I sprang off the balcony and darted up across the roof tiles to the peak. I skipped along the top, then leaped off.

Whoosh! I glided through the air and came down running on the next peak. Speeding across, I jumped to a low tower, then to a little dome.

Fwit-fwit-fwit! From one roof to the next, I flitted and danced, twirling in midair, flying across the tiles for a moment, then leaping onto the next rooftop.

This power had just come to me, too.

Quickening my pace, I jumped one last time, landed on the giant dome of the main palace, slid down, and dropped to its large balcony. It overlooked the city square and the sea beyond.

I saw people running in the courtyard below, calling out wildly. Shaggy six-legged pilkas clomped in every direction. And there, in the middle of it all, was something that chilled me to the bone.

A car.

With a long yellow body, eight fat tires, twin silver horns on either side, and a glass bubble on top, it was a car I had seen before.

My stomach tightened.

"Sparr's car!" I gasped. "He *is* here!"

Already my hands were hot. I didn't know how Sparr had gotten into the city, but I knew I'd have to join my parents to battle him out again. I only hoped that when my sparks flared, we would all be a match for him.

Gritting my teeth, I turned, crossed the balcony, slammed through the giant doors, and strode into the throne room.

"Sparr —" I shouted. I stopped.

Against the bright silver and green banners, the evil sorcerer stood alone in a circle of dark light.

One of his hands was raised high, clasped tightly in a fist. A sizzling spray of red sparks shot from it.

"Where are my parents?" I demanded.

Slowly, Sparr turned his head. His face was thin, his nose sharp, his eyes flashing like black flames. But it was the dark red fin behind each ear that proved he was not like the rest of us.

"Your parents are . . . sleeping in," he said softly, pointing to the end of the throne room.

My heart nearly stopped. There, inside a large crystal box, standing silent and unmoving, were my mother and father.

I ran to the box. "What did you do to them?" My parents' eyes were shut as if they were in a deep sleep. "Sparr, answer me!"

"They were in my way," said the sorcerer. "Or, I should say . . . *our* way."

"Our way?" I turned back to Sparr. "You can't be in the city. How did you even get in here?"

A cold smile crossed his lips. "Why, Keeah . . . don't you remember?"

I trembled. "Remember what?"

"How you kindly opened the gates for me!"

Red light sizzled from his closed hand.

"What? I'd never do that. I couldn't do that. I'm a wizard —"

"Oh?" he said. "And do wizards turn their palace guards into . . . *toads*?"

He motioned behind him. Several helmets on the floor toppled over. Under each was a big brown lump. They croaked one after the other, then hopped away.

"I didn't!" I said. "I was sleeping —"

"How nice, then, that *my* dreams came true!" said Sparr. "Because you gave me — this."

He opened his gloved fist and lifted his palm to me. In it sat a large crimson jewel, lighting up his face with a bright red glow.

I shivered. "The Red Eye of Dawn! But who — how did you — that's impossible —"

Turning, I saw the large iron door behind my father's throne hanging open. The small room inside was empty.

My head throbbed. My mouth felt dry.

"Sparr, I don't know what tricks you're playing here, but you won't get away with this!"

"I'm *not* getting away," he said calmly. "I'm staying right here. With your parents no longer a problem, Jaffa City is mine. You are mine. Oh, now look —"

Wham! The doors flew open.

Max charged in, his orange hair wild and standing straight up, his eyes wide and afraid. "Princess, creatures are pouring out of the Dark Lands. Ninns are sailing to the city right now. Sparr is taking over! We must fight —"

Without wanting to, I felt my hands moving up from my sides, growing hot. "Max, I . . ."

The spider troll stumbled to a halt. "Princess?"

Poooom! — a flash of sparks left my fingers. Max flew across the floor, blasting out the doors and over the balcony as if he were dragged away by an invisible rope.

A second later, he vanished out to sea.

"Max, no, no! My gosh, what have I done?!" I looked at the sparks spitting from the tips of my fingers.

They were jagged and hot and . . . red.

"Witch powers!" I gasped.

Sparr howled with laughter. "Ninns *are* coming here. Creatures from the Dark Lands *are* on the move. I *am* taking over. And all because of you, Keeah. Your dark powers — your *witch* powers — have finally come out! There's no one to stop me anymore. What a perfect moment. *Perfect!*"

I could barely speak. "Perfect? It's not perfect. It's the opposite of perfect. . . . It's . . . it's . . ."

Sparr turned to my parents' empty thrones and offered me his hand. "Now that you are a witch, Keeah, let's rule Droon as I had always hoped — *together!*"

Two

Ninth Orbit, Second Moon

I felt as cold as ice. I stared at my fingers. They sprayed red-hot sparks in the air.

"I didn't mean to do this. I *can't* do this!"

Sparr smiled, still waiting for me to take his hand. "But you did do it, Keeah. I have waited so long for your dark side to rise up and take over! Now, tell me. Jaffa City sounds so old-fashioned. What do you think of *Sparrville* —"

"Sparrville¿!"

I couldn't believe it. Here I was, standing inches from the worst sorcerer in Droon, all black clothes and red fire, but instead of blasting him, I had just zapped away my dearest friend!

"No. No! NO!" I yelled.

Sparr smirked. "Oh, I see. I suppose you like *Keeahport* better? Or perhaps . . . *Princesstown?*"

I backed away.

I knew what I had to do.

Keeping my arms at my sides and closing my eyes, I saw my parents' faces before me, as gentle and kind as they were last night.

I spoke the words my mother had taught me.

"*Blibby . . . blobby . . . snoo!*"

Sparr's face twisted. "Eh? I thought you were done with those silly spells — oh!"

Kkkkrrreeeekkkk! Everything in the

room, in the palace, in the whole city, stopped moving.

Everything went still.

Sparr stood there as motionless as a statue. His black eyes stared ahead. One of his hands still clasped the jewel while the other reached for me. His fins burned a deep red.

"You . . . horrible . . . *thing!*" I shouted.

Wiping my cheeks, I faced my parents, asleep in their crystal box. "Mother, you taught me this halting charm. Father, I have twelve hours before everything moves again in Jaffa City. Twelve hours to figure out how I let Sparr in, to find Max, to wake you both, to save Droon! My friends will come. Together, we'll fix this. We will!"

The sound of my footsteps echoed down the hall as I left the throne room.

Up the main staircase I ran, pounding up the marble steps two at a time. I raced through my father's library, up the final set of stairs, and into the corridor outside my room.

I paused to catch my breath.

In the stillness around me, I heard only the sound of my heart beating.

I felt so completely alone.

Peering for a moment out a small window, I saw the vast sea where I had sent Max. Its dark, booming waves suddenly brought up a name I hadn't thought of since last night.

"Demither!"

Demither was my mother's sister and the ruler of a powerful sea empire.

Demither was also a witch.

"Is it true, then? Am I becoming like her?"

Oooo — oooo. A low sound drifted up from the stairs. It was as if the wind were moaning through every silent room and open door of the palace.

I shook my head to clear it. "It's only the wind. And I have only twelve hours. Come on!"

I rushed into my room and quickly bolted the door behind me. Turning, I reached for the glass ball hanging in the air and pulled it down.

My heart leaped to remember how many times Eric, Julie, and Neal had dropped what they were doing to come and help me.

"Friends," I said, shaking, "my parents are under a spell. Sparr is here. I cursed poor Max! I need you now. Please hurry!"

I rolled my hand over the ball, and it lit up as if there were a fire inside it. Taking a feather pen, I formed a letter on the ball.

I nearly laughed to think how Galen would scold me if he saw how shaky my writing was.

"Wizards should have excellent handwriting," he told me once. "Power comes from words, both spoken *and* written. Remember that!"

Lifting my pen to the ball again, I wrote the letters slowly, starting from the end of the word and finishing at the beginning.

Ɛ . . . m . . . o . . . c

I paused, then added a second word.

Ɛ . . . s . . . a . . . e . . . l . . . p

I'm not sure I needed it, but my father always taught me to be polite. His Rules for the Kingly Art of Combat flashed through my mind.

1. Straighten your tunic before entering battle.

2. Always say, "May Droon be with you!" if your opponent sneezes.

3. No matter who wins, don't forget to offer your enemy a ride home.

I swallowed hard as I remembered his gruff voice reciting those rules. I set down the pen.

After a moment or two, the letters faded. The ball went clear.

"Okay," I said. "Now I wait —"

But right then, I saw a purple object sticking out from under my bed.

"My Wizardbook."

I picked it up and opened it. A lump formed in my throat as I remembered the first time I had ever seen the book.

Last night . . .

* * *

Fwoosh! Blam! Whizzz! Bright blue sparks were whizzing around my room in the twilight air. I spun near the ceiling for minutes at a time, sending objects flying wildly around me.

Knock, knock! I jumped to my bed as the door opened. My mother stepped in, wearing a long white gown. Behind her was my father in full armor, his twin-horned helmet on his head.

Between them was tiny Max. His wild hair was combed flat, and he was wiggling as if ready to burst into song.

"What is it?" I asked.

"Keeah, do you know what tomorrow is?" asked my father.

I thought for a moment. "Is it my turn to walk the pilkas again?"

He laughed. "No, dear! Max, if you please."

"Ahem!" The spider troll cleared his throat and unrolled a small scroll.

In a voice as deep as he could make it, Max began, "My dear princess, tomorrow is the first day of the seventh month before the last week nearest the fourth hour of the third season following the ninth orbit of the second moon!"

I think I must have frowned.

"In other words," said my mother, laughing as she brought out a package from behind her gown, "open it!"

I gasped. "A present? For me? I knew I liked the ninth orbit of the second moon!"

I tore off the paper. Inside, I found a small book covered in rich purple leather. Gold designs coiled across its shiny finish. A hazy silver stone set right in the center of the cover shone with threads of red and blue light twisting deeply within it.

"It's so beautiful," I said. "Thank you!"

"Keeah, this is not just any book," my mother said, sitting on my bed. "It is your Wizardbook. A moment comes to every wizard when your magic becomes greater than it has ever been —"

"It's like a growth spurt!" said Max.

I gazed at the objects floating above us.

"That moment is coming," my mother said. "Your Wizardbook is your story of how you become a *droomar* wizard."

"*Droomar!*" I whispered.

"Yes, *droomar!*" boomed my father. "Even before Galen, the mysterious *droomar* were living in caves, keeping alive the ancient wisdom of Droon. They are a magical elfin sort of folk —"

"But I'm not an elf," I said. "How can I become a *droomar?*"

My mother smiled. "Elfin Sight," she said. "It is a power given to you at the moment you need it most. With the Sight, you see our world as you never have before."

"It is a wizard's secret weapon," said my father. "Elfin Sight is the true mark of a *droomar*."

"And a sign of great love," my mother said.

Max patted my shoulder. "The queen traveled a thousand miles in a single day to find her deepest magic," he said. "An old *droomar* was her guide. That was a dangerous journey!"

"At every step I was tempted by the darker ways," she said. "I had many friends with me, including your aunt, my sister. Finally, I was alone —"

She paused, looking out my window to the sea beyond the city walls.

My aunt. Her sister. Demither.

The Sea Witch.

I shivered to remember how, like my mother, Demither was born to do great magic — *droomar* magic — until Sparr tempted her to join him.

From the moment she became his servant, she couldn't rebel against him. She had to help in his plans to take over Droon.

I remembered, too, how once, when I was very young and far from home, Demither shared her powers with me. I remembered how her red sparks flowed into me, and how happy I was when those dark powers seemed to go away.

"Is Demither a *droomar?*" I asked.

My father shook his head. "The day she turned away from her family was the day she lost her Elfin Sight."

My mother looked at me again. "Keeah, let your Wizardbook inspire you. You alone can tell your story. When you come to write it, I know you will fill these pages with the wonderful language of your soul!"

It was true — the blank white pages seemed to call out to be filled with magical words.

"Thank you," I said.

"Soon you'll be a true *droomar* like your mother," said my father proudly. "Keeah, your moment is nearly here!"

Nearly here.

I remember the thrill of hearing that.

Now, as the memory of their late-night visit faded, and the wind howled in the halls again, I couldn't deny it anymore.

"I might be a wizard," I murmured, "but so was Demither once. When my big moment comes, maybe it won't be like anyone expects. Maybe my true powers *are* coming out. And they're not *droomar* powers. Maybe I'm a —"

Ooooo — The sound echoed up the stairs.

I felt a chill on my neck.

"That's not the wind," I said. "It's a voice. . . ."

"*Oooo* —" The moan sounded closer.

"It's the voice of . . . a ghost!"

Without saying a word or thinking a thought — *zzzz!* — my hands flashed red, and the bucket I had flown the night before was hovering before me, brimming with cold water.

"*Oooo* —" The sound came closer still.

I gulped down my fear and grabbed the bucket. "So there's a ghost, is there? Well, witch powers or not, if it comes here, it'll get a wet head!"

Leaping to a chair, I carefully balanced

the bucket on the edge of the door frame.

"If ghosts even *have* heads!"

I braced myself, staring at the door, both hands sprinkling bright red sparks.

Suddenly — *shooom!* — the little fireplace behind me exploded with a giant cloud of smoke.

I whirled around to see legs and arms and sneakers shooting straight at me.

I gasped. "Eric?"

"Out — of — the — way!" he cried.

Three

Chitchat with a Hat

Blam! Wump! Oooof! Eric flew like a shot across the room, hurtling me back to the bed.

"Sorry!" he yelled. "We — uh — fell!"

Julie thudded down the fireplace shaft, leaped to her feet, then collapsed to the floor. "*Owww!*"

"Way to be in the way!" said Neal. He tumbled over Julie, struck my bookcase, rolled back, flipped once, slammed against the wall, then stopped.

Dazed, he looked up. "Oh, Keeah . . . hi!"

"I'm so glad you're here!" I said, rushing to help them up.

Eric stared at the fireplace, wobbling back and forth. "Lucky you didn't have a fire!"

"Neal would have put it out anyway," said Julie. She stepped over the puddle at Neal's feet. He was soaking wet.

Neal laughed. "Water balloons!" he said. "When you called us, I was filling them to throw at Julie and Eric. But they kept exploding."

"The water balloons kept exploding," said Eric. "The magic word being *water*. Neal was drenched —" He stopped. "Keeah, you look worried. What's happening? Why did you call us here?"

There were so many things to tell. But when I opened my mouth, I couldn't make myself say any of them. I just pointed out to my balcony.

They saw the square full of people and animals, all silent and still.

"Holy cow!" gasped Neal. "Everyone has become statues? What's going on?"

"It's a halting spell," I said. "Every person and creature in Jaffa City has stopped moving for twelve hours. I had to do it. Because of Sparr. Because . . . he's here. . . ."

Julie's jaw dropped. "Sparr's here? How did he even get this far? Who let him into the city? What does he want?"

I swallowed hard. There was only one answer.

"Me, me, and, I guess, me . . ."

Holding back the tears as best I could, I told them everything. That Sparr had put my parents under a spell, that he said I let him through the gates and gave him the Red Eye of Dawn, and that I cursed Max far away across the sea.

"It's all because," I said, forcing myself to say it, "I'm turning into a witch. Just like Demither did. The dark powers she gave me once are coming back. They're growing in me."

To show them, I opened my hands. Red sparks glowed from the tips of my fingers.

"To make things worse, a huge army of Ninns is on its way," I said finally. "And creatures from the Dark Lands. It's happening. Sparr is taking over —"

Eric stared at me for a second, then shook his head. "I don't believe it. Somebody's playing tricks here. Maybe even Demither, trying to win you over. This must be some weirdo evil plan."

"Besides," said Julie, "you used a wizard spell to halt things, right? And you called us to come. So you're not totally a — you know."

Neal frowned. "Plus, letting Sparr just stroll right into your home? I don't think so —"

"*Oooooo!*" came the sound from the hall.

Everyone went quiet.

"And there's that," I whispered.

Neal gulped. "*That?* What exactly *is* that?"

"A ghost, I think," I said. "It's haunting me."

"A ghost! Why didn't you tell us?" said Eric. Bright silver sparks began to sprinkle from his fingers. "Stand back, everyone. We'll stop it where it stands. Or hovers. Or whatever!"

"*Oooo — oooo — eeeee — kkkk — ohhh!*"

As we watched, something big and brown and rumpled pushed itself right through the wall and into the room with us.

It floated three feet above the floor.

It had a wide, floppy brim.

It was a hat.

"*Oooo-oooo-oooo!*" said a voice from a few inches below where the hat was floating.

Julie blinked. "The ghost is . . . a *hat?*"

"Thum!" said the space under the hat. "Augustus Rudolphus Septimus Thum! At your service. Yes, yes, I know. Big name, tiny body —"

"We don't see a body," said Neal.

"Of course you don't see a . . . What did you say?"

"All we see is a hat," said Julie.

"All you see is — oh, dear, I'm so forgetful!" The hat wiggled, twirled once, and dipped backward.

Plooop! In the space below it appeared a small, white, four-footed creature, standing upright. He had a stubby snout, bushy whiskers, green eyes, and pointed ears. He was wearing blue spectacles tied on a ribbon. He bowed with a flourish.

When he did, I saw through him slightly.

"There!" said the creature. He cleared his throat. "Now then. I'm not a ghost, no, but a *droomar*. That's a *drrr*, and an *oooo*, and a *marrrrr* —"

I gasped. "My mother is a *droomar* wizard!"

"*Oooo,* I know," said the creature, wiggling his nose. "And I am your guide. Well, sort of. I've come to give you a message. Now then, what was it? Oh, yes. *Booooooo* —"

"Now, stop that!" said Julie, her hands on her hips. "Why are you haunting poor Keeah?"

The creature let out a big gasp. "Haunting? Goodness, no! *Booo* was just the first part of what I have to say. The rest of the message is . . . is . . . oh. Oh, now I've forgotten. Wait. *Boogie dune!*"

We looked at him.

"Or, no," he said. "That's not it. *Beagle drum!* No, no . . . *Baggy dome . . . ?*"

"*Bagel Town!*" said Neal, lighting up.

"That doesn't sound right," said Thum.

"Could it be . . . *Bangledorn?*" I asked.

"THAT'S IT!" Thum shouted. "Bangledorn! The Bangledorn Forest! Where the Bangledorn monkeys live! You must go there at once!"

Julie frowned. "Go to Bangledorn? But Sparr is right here in the palace. The Bangledorn Forest is a long way away. Why should we go there?"

Thum grumbled. "Yes, well, you would have to ask me that. . . ."

I clasped the Wizardbook. "I know! My mother's wizard journey took her a long way. Maybe this is part of my *droomar* journey —"

The elfin creature jumped. "Mother's journey? Wizardbook? Now I remember!"

He waved a little paw over my book's silvery stone. An instant later, the haze cleared and it showed the image of a thick green forest.

Neal gasped. "It's like a tiny TV!"

Eeeee — eeee! A high-pitched shriek rang out from the stone. Then we saw dozens of tiny green monkeys fleeing through the trees.

"Something's happening," said Eric.

A moment later, we saw a mass of black wings. Finally, we saw the red fur, rusty armor, and glinting claws of an army flying into the forest.

"Oh, my gosh!" gasped Julie. "Wing-wolves!"

We knew wingwolves. We had battled one before. It was a terrifying creature from an ancient tribe that Galen called the Hakoth-Mal.

"So, it's true," I said. "Sparr's creatures *are* coming from the Dark Lands. If this is part of my journey, it's up to me to stop them!"

"It's up to *us*," said Eric. "Together."

Thum grinned. "Yes, yes, that's the message! Go! And remember this — Droon's future lies with the one who has the biggest head!"

"The biggest head?" said Julie. "What does that mean? You know, Thum, for someone who can be invisible, you're not very clear —"

"I am now!" said the *droomar*.

A moment later — *pooomf!* — he was gone.

Neal stared at the empty spot. "Could the guy have *been* any weirder? Wait. Let me answer that. No, he could not."

Eric laughed. "But he showed us that Bangledorn's in trouble. We need to go. Come on!"

For the first time since I woke up, I felt myself smile.

I had just remembered my mother's words.

I had many friends with me.

"Okay, then," I said, tucking my Wizardbook into a leather pouch and hooking it on my belt. "Maybe we *can* change things. To the forest, everybody. And Sparr will take us there!"

I pointed down from my balcony to the yellow car. Its fat tires pointed to the city gate.

Neal grinned. "We are gonna travel in style! And I wanna drive!"

He charged over to the door. That's when I remembered the bucket. "Neal, wait, no —"

Sploooosh! A gallon of icy cold water dropped over him, soaking him completely.

"I am so sorry!" I said, trying not to laugh.

Neal stood there, dripping onto the floor and staring at us. "Just when I was starting to dry out, too," he said. "Nice. Very nice. . . ."

Flight ✶f the Wingy W✶lves

Racing outside, we dashed across the square to the long yellow car.

"It looks super fast," said Eric, lifting the bubble top. "There's a map here, but no steering wheel. How does it work?"

"It's magical," I said. "Galen told me it goes where Sparr commands it to go. And it goes fast."

"That's why *I* should drive," said Neal.

Eric turned. "You? Why you?"

"Because I love fast cars," said Neal. "Besides, I'm pretty sure I'm the tallest." He brushed his wet hair up on his forehead.

"But I'm a week older," said Eric.

"We're all getting older!" said Julie, leaping into the driver's seat. "And we're wasting time. Car, to the Bangledorn Forest!"

The moment we jumped in — *ooga!* — the horns blared, and we screeched out the courtyard gates and away from the silent palace.

"The journey begins," I said. "Mother, Father, I'll do everything I can to stop Sparr. I promise."

"We promise," said Eric. "Droon is important to us, too."

Neal nodded. "Plus, how often do you get to freeze Old Fishfins and stop his creepy plans?"

"And we *will* stop him," said Julie.

"Thanks," I said.

But as the car leaped away from Jaffa City, bumping and twisting toward the plains of middle Droon, I saw black clouds forming on the distant horizon.

What Sparr had said was already happening.

Creatures were coming from the Dark Lands.

He was taking over.

I only hoped I wasn't helping him.

We zigzagged through the countryside, with Julie driving first, then Neal. We raced faster and faster. Sparr's car seemed to know which roads to take.

Finally, we wove through the plains and rose over the crest of a giant hill. We slowed.

"There it is," I said.

In front of us stood the huge mass of

the Bangledorn Forest. It stretched all the way to the border of the smoky Dark Lands.

Neal drove up and stopped where two giant oak trees soared over a path leading inside.

"It looks peaceful," said Julie. "And magical."

"Except it's neither," said Eric. "Wing-wolves are in there. Plus, we can't use our powers here."

For ages, the Bangledorn Forest has been one of the few places in Droon where no magic is allowed. Luckily, my fingers weren't sparking.

"I'll try my best," I said. "Julie?"

She looked at a small scar on her hand. It was where a wingwolf had scratched her, giving her the power to fly. "No flying. I promise."

"I guess we can't use magical cars, either," said Neal. "We'll have to go in on foot."

We all got out and entered the forest slowly. It was hushed and cool around us, but the birds that usually greeted us were silent. And the sky above was getting darker by the minute.

"Bangledorn City is this way," I said.

But the moment I took a step — *fwish-fwish!* — a thick net of vines swept around us. It pulled us instantly into the high branches.

"Hey! We're trapped!" said Neal, struggling.

"Magic or not," said Eric, "I'll blast us out —"

"Oh!" hissed a voice. "It's Princess Keeah!"

As we dangled upside down, we saw

two furry green faces peering down through the leaves.

I gasped. "Wait, Twee, is that you?"

"And Woot?" said Julie.

It was the tiny brother and sister monkeys we had met on an earlier adventure. They jumped with surprise and hurried down to us.

"Forgive us!" chirped Twee, quickly untying the net and leading us out to a thick branch. "We thought you were the enemy. Wingwolves have invaded our forest!"

"And chased us from our homes," said Woot.

"They're moving in," added a third voice.

We looked up. A tall figure in a blue cape swung down silently from above. She wore a crown of purple leaves on her head.

"Queen Ortha," I said, bowing. "We

came as soon as we heard —" In the leaves beyond her, I saw the faces of hundreds of monkeys, their eyes huge with fear.

Ortha put a finger to her lips. "Follow me!"

Grabbing a thick vine, she slipped away quietly. We followed, swinging on vine after vine, until we landed on a branch overlooking Bangledorn City.

Houses of all sizes were built among the curling branches around us. Vine bridges dangled between them. And in the center, largest of all, was the many-leveled palace of the queen.

But crawling over every inch of the city, leaping from house to house, flying among the trees, were furry red warriors with long claws.

"We are not a fighting people," whispered Ortha. "But to see them take over our homes . . ."

Neal grumbled. "No kidding. One wing-wolf is bad enough. They brought the whole family!"

From the moment I saw the terrible creatures, I felt my hands growing hot. Words began swimming in my head, like the ones that woke me that morning.

My eyelids felt heavy. I closed my eyes. *"Pen-ga . . . zo . . ."*

Zzzzz! My eyes shot open, and I saw my fingertips spark suddenly.

So did Ortha. "Keeah . . . those words. They sound like the ancient language of Goll. How do you know them?"

I looked around. Twee and Woot were staring, too. "I'm sorry . . . this morning . . . I . . ."

I explained everything that had happened, and how I was acting so strangely.

"I must have let Sparr into the city," I

said. "I don't really remember. He told me his creatures would come. I think my new powers are behind it all."

Ortha frowned. "When Queen Relna took her wizard journey, it was also a dangerous time."

"But what are we going to do?" asked Eric.

I looked out at the wingwolves, then at the distant forest, then at my sparking hands. I knew I wouldn't be able to control them for long.

"Maybe there's a way. . . ." I said.

Ortha nodded. A small smile came to her lips. "First, the wingwolves need to know they aren't welcome here."

Twee glanced at his sister. "How about some nuts?" He chuckled.

Neal blinked. "A snack before fighting? Cool phase one. I like how you guys think."

"Not a snack," said Twee. Giggling, he and Woot leaped away with all the other monkeys.

A moment later, they were back, carrying mounds of small, shiny nuts.

"These nuts are only good for one thing," said Woot.

"To make a wingwolf think twice about trying to move in!" Twee added.

My hands were growing hotter by the second. "Phase two is up to me," I said.

While everyone took nuts and quietly surrounded the city, I moved carefully out to the edge of a long branch.

When we were in position, Ortha gave a loud shout. *"O — lee — lee!"*

Thonk! Flang! Whizzz! The hard nuts rained down on the wingwolves.

"Gaaaakkkk!" The creatures roared as the nuts struck their big furry heads and their giant clawed feet. They leaped for

cover, bumping into one another, catching their wings, and falling.

"Take that!" yelled Eric.

"Nuts for the nuts!" cried Julie.

"Now phase two," I said. "This is my job —"

I leaped from the end of the branch and grabbed a vine. While my friends kept hurling nuts, I swung away through the trees.

As I had hoped, the Hakoth-Mal saw my sparks. More and more of them flitted through the air after me. When I swung to the ground, I dashed between the trees until I flew out of the forest.

I turned to the Hakoth-Mal. "I can use magic here!" I aimed my hands, my sparks flaring.

Then I spoke. *"Pen-ga . . . zo . . . thool!"*

The air rang suddenly with shrieks and howls.

But instead of diving at me, the creatures flashed their claws and flew higher, then higher.

I didn't understand the words that I heard in my head, but I knew what they meant to the wingwolves. "Go away!"

The creatures howled again and again even as the sound of their flapping wings grew faint.

I searched the sky until I couldn't see them anymore.

They were lost in the dark air.

The wingwolves were gone.

"*O — lee — lee!*" A cheer rose from the forest. A crowd of monkeys came running out to us, led by Eric, Neal, and Julie.

"You beat them," said Eric. "They're gone."

I couldn't stop trembling. "The wingwolves are gone. But I didn't beat them. I think . . . I just . . . sent them away. And the journey isn't over. I heard them talking."

"You heard them?" said Eric. "All they do is grunt and growl — when they're not attacking!"

"Don't ask me how, but I understood their words," I said. "More monsters are coming from the Dark Lands. To a place called Rivertangle."

"Let me guess," said Julie. "It's not a cool water park, is it?"

"Please don't mention water," said Neal.

Ortha smiled. "No. Rivertangle is a place where five rivers come together. It is near the deserts of Lumpland. Keeah, I told you your mother's journey was dangerous. You helped our forest. Perhaps now I can help you. I will come."

"Our queen will go with Keeah!" yelled Twee. "I will come, too. And Woot, too!"

"But my powers," I said. "The red sparks —"

"Red sparks. Blue sparks," said Woot. "We love green most of all!"

Eric grinned. "It looks like our troop is growing. Good thing we have a big car!"

It turned out to be even bigger than we thought. When Ortha, Woot, and Twee climbed in, the long yellow car amazingly stretched out even longer, adding another whole row of seats.

"Car — to Rivertangle!" yelled Eric.

Together there were seven of us as we roared away from the forest.

Mile after mile, we rumbled south across the plains. It wasn't long before I heard words in my head again.

But this time I wasn't the only one who heard them.

"Keeah, your pouch!" said Woot. "Look!"

The Wizardbook's stone was glowing.

I pulled out the book. In the stone, we saw what looked like waves moving wildly on a vast blue sea.

Crouching closer, we spied an enormous ship, its dirty sails billowing with wind. It sailed along a rocky shore ahead of many smaller ships.

On the side of the hull was a single word:

Stinkenpoop

"Oh, my gosh," I said. "That's a Ninn ship —"

"And I know that coastline," said Ortha. "They're sailing north . . . to Jaffa City."

"Sparr really is trying to take over!" said Eric.

The image on the stone closed in on a

fat barrel lashed to the main mast. As the ship drove over the waves, the barrel's top wobbled slightly, and a head popped up from inside.

A head covered with messy orange hair.

I jumped. "It's Max! He's all right!"

My heart beat wildly to see Max again. He glanced around the ship carefully, then stopped. His mouth hung open. His eyes widened.

Then we saw what he was looking at.

The crew of chubby Ninns was leaning close together.

They slung their big arms around one another.

And they began to sing.

Five

On the Bad Ship Stinkenpoop

Yo-ho-ho! Yo-ho-ho!
We grunt and pull the heavy oar
  across the seas that splash and spill!
We sail and sail and sail some more
  to our new home in Spa-arrville!

We listened in shock as the warriors grunted and growled their song.

"Sparrville?" Neal snorted. "Yeah, I don't think so! Not with Max standing in your way. Well, okay, he's hiding in a barrel, but still!"

As Eric followed the map, zooming the yellow car through the grassy plains, the Wizardbook's stone showed us what was happening on the ship.

Ninns lurched across the deck, some dragging ropes, some hauling giant cartons, still others clambering up the rigging to trim the ship's sails.

As they did, Max turned carefully around in the barrel, spying everything.

"Well, well," we heard him whisper. "Of all the places I could have been sent, it had to be here."

"I'm so sorry, Max!" I whispered, wishing he could hear me.

A cluster of Ninns plodded by the barrel and climbed to a crooked wheel on an upper deck.

A smile crossed Max's lips. He blinked

his eyes and twitched his nose. "One spider troll, lots of Ninns? Seems about right!"

Looking both ways, he gripped the sides of the barrel and was out in a flash. Leaning back in for a moment, he came out with four of his eight paws clutching plump yellow bananas.

Neal grumbled as we raced along. "Why do I never eat before I come to Droon? I can practically smell those bananas."

Max chuckled. "Ninns may like to sail, but they also like fruit! Let's see how much!"

"He's got a plan," said Julie. "Go, Max!"

Peeling one of the bananas, Max darted behind a bundle of furniture — bedposts, a mattress, an armchair, a twisted lamp, and a cradle.

"They really want to set up shop in Jaffa City," said Eric. "Don't worry, Keeah. They won't."

Max looked around. "Spider trolls," he whispered. "Orange hair, people think. Big noses, people think. Furry and cuddly, people think!"

He giggled suddenly. "True enough. But when we are pushed to the limit, watch out. I'll stop this ship. And the whole Ninn army, too!"

"Yay, Max!" Twee cheered. "But be careful!"

Max tossed the empty peel near the barrel. Opening another banana, he tossed its peel not far away.

"And here they come!" he whispered.

Two large Ninns stomped heavily up to the barrel and popped it open.

They blinked.

"Empty!" the first one growled. "Sparr said treats. How do we sail with no treats?"

Max giggled, peeling and eating a third

banana. "What can I say? When I'm hungry — I eat!"

"I wish I could," whispered Neal.

The second Ninn kept staring into the barrel, frowning. "I only came for treats. And to help Sparr fight the baddies and take over."

The first Ninn snorted. "*We're* the baddies."

"Well, *you* are!" said the second Ninn.

"No, you."

"Nuh-uh, YOU!" He pushed hard, sending the other Ninn back onto one of the banana peels.

Wump! The red warrior thundered to the deck in a heap. "I get you!" he roared.

He kicked out, and the second Ninn slipped on the other peel and landed faceup.

"*Owww!*"

That's when a dozen more Ninns stumbled up from below. They spotted Max's hiding place and began shouting. "Get the furry rat!"

"Rat? Rat!" said Max. "Well, I never ever heard such a thing. . . . *Rat?* Well, follow this rat!"

He leaped to the mattress, bounced once, and flung himself into the rigging. Then he clambered up to the very tip of the giant mast.

"Get him!" shouted the Ninns.

The warriors on the upper deck charged up after him, leaving the ship's wheel spinning.

The thick ropes sagged under the Ninns' weight. The ship began to wobble on the waves.

Even as the Ninns followed, Max scampered across the rigging as if it were a spiderweb.

"I must get to the wheel!" he shouted.

"Must help Keeah! Turn — ship — from Jaffa City!"

"He's amazing!" said Julie. "Even against all those Ninns, he can do anything!"

"And he hasn't lost faith in me," I said.

"Of course not!" said Twee.

"Who could ever?" said Eric.

My heart raced to hear them say that.

Max sprayed a stream of spider silk at the Ninns, snaring them in a thick web.

More red warriors climbed up from below. They followed Max over the rigging until he had all of them tangled in his spidery goop!

The Ninns howled. They shouted. They shook their fists. But they were stuck to the rigging.

"Yahoo!" cried Eric. "Take *that*, Sparr!"

Max laughed at the tangled Ninns. "I was going to ask for help sailing the ship, but I see you are all tied up! Now, watch this!"

Clutching the top of the mainsail, Max dug his paws into it and slid down to the deck, tearing the sail in two all the way down.

"Hey! Way to go!" shouted Neal.

"He is a great little warrior," said Ortha.

With its sail ripped and its wheel spinning, the giant ship twisted in the wind. The smaller ships behind it began to follow it in circles.

Max stormed up to the ship's wheel. "Galen always told me of the power of words! Well, here's a word you Ninns won't forget — Max! That's me! How's that for a *yo-ho-ho* — oh!"

Suddenly, the hull rose on a wave and the ship went careening toward the shore. It lurched straight at the rocks that lined the coast.

"Oh, dear, dear!" cried the spider troll. "I fibbed! I can't really sail a ship! Someone, please help! Oh, Galen! Oh, Keeah! Oh, help!"

"He's in trouble!" shouted Woot. "Max!"

"Don't they have a brake on that thing?" said Neal.

The ship began spinning quickly. Giant waves broke over the deck, driving the ship right at the jagged rocks.

Max pulled the wheel. "Keeah — good thing you taught me to swim — oh!"

"Max!" I shouted.

Krrkk! The hull struck the rocks and cracked.

"*Stinkenpoop* sinking!" cried one Ninn.

"Ninns — wet!" boomed a second.

As wave upon wave crashed over the ship, they seemed to splash against the inside of the Wizardbook's stone, washing away the scene.

"Max! Max!" I said. "This is all my fault —"

"He'll be okay," said Julie. "He has to be. He's . . . Max."

Eric nodded. "If anyone can escape a shipwreck and a bunch of Ninns, he can. I know he will."

"I know it, too," said Ortha. "But right now, look. We're here!"

In a valley just ahead were the blue waters of several rivers, twisting and splashing together.

"Rivertangle," said Twee. "We found it —"

"We found them, too," said Neal, pointing up.

Three dark shapes swooped down from the massing clouds and flew over Rivertangle.

As we raced closer we saw their scaly skin and giant heads. We saw their pointed red noses, whiskers, long gray hair, blazing eyes, and broken teeth. We'd seen the creepy creatures before.

"Haggons!" I whispered. "Hag dragons fresh from the Dark Lands. What do they want here?"

Twee jumped straight up. "Look in the river!"

Bobbing in the wild water was a boat. Inside, flailing wildly with a tiny oar, was what looked like a small purple pillow.

"Khan!" I said. "It's the King of the Lumpies!"

The haggons pointed their claws at the boat, and the largest one cackled, "I smell lunch!"

"Our last meal was hours ago!" growled the second.

"And I need my beauty snack!" said the third.

"No, you don't!" said Eric. "Car! Go! Now!"

But as we roared to the river, the ugly sisters dived at Khan, shrieking their own terrible call.

"Haggons! Attack! Now!"

Six

Follow the Leader

Ooga! The car's eight tires shot waves of dust behind us, and we raced even faster.

"They're almost at the river!" yelled Julie.

"Haggons, get lost!" shouted Eric. Silver sparks burst from his fingers. He fired. *Blam!*

The hag sisters ducked the blast and clacked their jaws angrily, but kept diving for Khan.

Angrily, I pounded the dashboard. "Faster!"

As if the car heard me — *floink!* — a small panel flipped down from the dashboard. On it were two buttons, one green, one yellow.

Suddenly, my fingers sparked red. The hag sisters must have seen it. They slowed their dive.

"Keeeeeahhhh!" gargled the lead haggon.

"Never mind her," cried Julie. "Press one!"

"Okay, but —" I pressed the yellow button.

Vrrr-rrrt! Two giant webbed fins, like Sparr's own, jutted from the back of the car. A second later, we shot straight up from the road.

"*Weeee!*" shouted Twee. "I like this!"

"Me, too," said Eric. "But we're on the

haggons' turf now. And they know how to fly!"

"Let me try —" I said.

Right, left, up, and down, I flew us away from the river into a range of hills. The haggons followed, but every time we thought we'd lost them, they swooped from behind another hill.

"Wherever we go, they're there!" cried Julie.

I drove the car straight up into the clouds. The haggons followed us. Then I circled around and around, but they stayed on our tail.

Faster and faster I drove, until the haggons' eyes began to spin around in their heads.

"Yes!" said Eric. "Keep doing that! Make them dizzy!"

I kept flying the car around until, finally, the three sisters pulled up short and began coughing. Their heads wobbled, and their wings drooped.

"Good, Keeah!" said Ortha. "Now, to Khan!"

I dipped the car below the clouds. Khan's boat was hurtling into the worst part of the river.

The crashing of giant waves nearly drowned out his calls for help.

"Press the green button!" cried Woot. "We love green!"

Vrrrrt! The fins on the back flipped in, and the car dived. Right into the water.

Sploosh! The tires became fatter, and long hulls slid out from under the car. We splashed down onto the lurching waters and raced to where Khan's boat was sinking under the waves.

"Oh, dear, help!" cried the little Lumpy king.

"Grab on!" I shouted. As we pulled up,

Khan jumped from his boat, landing softly in the car.

"Keeeeeaaaahh —" the haggons shrieked from beyond the clouds.

It was a sound that made me shiver. "Oh, no."

"Hey, I saw a movie once where people who were being chased hid in a tunnel," said Neal.

"Good idea, Neal!" said Khan. "There are tunnels all along Rivertangle!" He pointed to a cavern on the riverbank, hollowed out by the waves.

"So let's get out of here!" said Eric.

With the haggons still in the clouds, we raced to the tunnel and drove in. We stopped.

The tunnel was dark and quiet.

"Khan, are you okay?" whispered Julie.

"Only because of you!" he said, still huffing and puffing. "The hags attacked

Lumpland and chased me into Rivertangle. What is going on?"

"The dark powers are rising," I said. "Starting with me."

"It's happening all over Droon," said Twee.

"Hush now," said Ortha. "The haggons are close. Let them pass by."

We heard the flap of leathery wings.

And I heard words again. When I glanced at my fingertips, they were sprinkling red sparks. That's when it came to me.

"We can't hide," I said. "The haggons know where we are. Someone's telling them."

"Who?" asked Julie.

I breathed deeply. "Me."

"Princess, no!" Khan cried.

"I hear words in my head," I said. "Strange words of old magic. I don't know where they're coming from, but the haggons understand. It's like with the wing-wolves. Wait here."

I jumped from the car to a path running down the side of the tunnel.

"Keeah, where are you going?" asked Eric.

I didn't answer. When I got to the entrance, the three haggons were already there, flapping down over the water, flashing their claws.

I heard everyone gasp when I spoke.

"Plah — no — thloom."

Still hovering, the haggons bowed.

Then the largest of the three spoke. "What would you have us do . . . our princess?"

"Leave us alone," I said, my sparks flaring.

The three winged sisters grinned wide, toothless grins. Then they nodded their gray heads.

I finally understood what was going on. The haggons followed us because . . . I was their leader.

I could command them to do anything.

The sisters clustered together. Then they flapped their wings and leaped away into the air. A moment later, they were gone.

"That was awesome!" said Neal, running to me. "They didn't eat us. Not even a single bite!"

"Keeah, you saved us again!" said Twee.

I shook my head. "I only sent them away. I —"

My heart fluttered to see something appear three feet above the water.

It was a wrinkled brown hat.

"Thum!" I said, running to the hat. "It's Thum, everybody! Show yourself. Do you have a message for me?"

"Oooo, I do!" The *droomar*'s little face appeared under the hat. "And here it is. Oooo!"

"Thum, please!" said Julie. "What's the rest?"

". . . bja," he said, dangling his toes in the water. "*Oooo* first, *bja* second. Oooo . . . bja!"

Eric blinked. "Oobja? You mean the Oobja mole people ruled by Batamogi?"

"Who live in the Dust Hills of Panjibarrh?" asked Neal.

"Exactly!" said Thum. "The Panjibarrh of Batamogi ruled by the Dust Hills of Oobja. Or, rather, what you said. You need to go there."

"Why must Keeah go to Panjibarrh?" asked Ortha.

"Are more of Sparr's creatures attacking there?" I asked.

Thum splashed his toes and grinned.

"This time I know the answer. You must go there because the Oobja know what you need to know. Only, they don't know that they know what you need to know. Do you know what I mean?"

Julie frowned. "No."

Thum shrugged. "Then let me be as clear as possible. Like this —" *Pooomf!* He vanished in a big spray of water that splashed into the cave.

And right onto Neal.

He stared at the empty spot and grumbled.

"Even so, he told us where to go," said Ortha.

"And we only have a little time left," I said. "The halting spell is half over."

"Then let's go to Panjibarrh to see what the Oobja know," said Woot.

"And when you say us," added Khan, "I

certainly hope you mean me, too. For I am coming!"

"The pillow king will come!" said Woot.

"It will probably be dangerous," said Eric.

Khan fluffed his tassels. "I expected no less!"

I gave Khan a hug. "Thank you."

Moments later, the eight of us drove Sparr's even longer car out of the tunnel, splashing water high on both sides. Twee and Woot sat in the driver's seat with Ortha as we raced over the plains to Panjibarrh.

Panjibarrh. The Land of the Dust Hills.

The country that gets its name from the giant dust storms that rise suddenly out of nowhere.

Like the one that just then began to spin around our car.

And lift us off the ground.

Seven

What the Oobja Know

Whoosh-sh-sh! A giant funnel of dust whirled around us, lifting the car high in the air.

"Hold on tight!" shouted Ortha. "We're going up!"

Blam! Blam! I blasted the air with red sparks, but the dust storm just whirled faster and faster.

Eric sent a bright shower of silver light

from his hands. The wind only swept it away.

"We're doomed!" yelled Khan.

A moment later, the car jerked upside down. The glass dome flipped open, and we were thrown out while the car kept rising.

And we fell.

"Now we're *really* doomed!" Neal shouted.

"Grab one another!" cried Ortha. "Stay together!"

Julie clutched Eric's feet while Neal whirled upside down in the dust, clinging to Twee and Woot. Ortha, Khan, and I held one another tight.

"Brace yourselves!" I yelled.

A moment later — *plop! plop! plop!* — Eric, Julie, and I went slamming down into a hedge of brown bushes. Ortha, Khan,

Twee, and Woot landed in a soft mound of dust.

Neal missed the bushes and the dust.

He landed in a fountain.

Splash! Neal was drenched — again.

Jumping up, he shook himself, then looked at us.

"Don't even say it."

The storm whirled away as quickly as it had come. When it did, we could see that we were in a village of small mud homes. They were stacked one on top of another up the sides of big brown hills.

"Well, we're in Panjibarrh," Julie whispered. "I remember this village from the last time."

In the center of the village was a giant wheel made of thick planks of wood and lying flat on the ground like a big plate. A long wooden lever stuck up from its middle. The Oobja mole people used the wheel to make dust storms to protect against enemies.

Looking at my red sparks, I wondered if they would think *I* was an enemy.

"My princess!" called a voice.

We turned to see a small head with a large crown on it pop out from one of the huts.

"Batamogi?" I asked.

A short creature jumped from the door and ran to us. He had curling whiskers and pointy ears. He wore a green cape and a gold crown.

"Princess Keeah!" he shouted. Instantly, doors in the other mud huts opened and the village square filled with the furry folk called Oobja.

"We were so afraid," said Batamogi. "We sent the dust storm because of the yellow car. We thought you were the evil one, Lord Sparr himself!"

"We just borrowed his car," said Neal, looking up in the clouds. "It's still spinning around up there somewhere."

Batamogi took us into his small hut. Huddling by a fire, we told him everything that had happened since morning. Even about my powers.

"A *droomar* told you to come here?" said Batamogi, his eyes wide. "But I don't know anything. All I've seen are black clouds moving over the plains and getting thicker all the time!"

"The *droomar* said you know something," I said. "But you don't know that you know."

Batamogi frowned. "Not knowing there is a secret is the most secret kind of secret. Let me see. . . . Sometimes I get tired of all the dust. No one knows that. . . . I broke my brother's wagon when I was three. . . . And then there's — what's *that?*"

A glow shone from the pouch on my belt.

"My Wizardbook!" I said, taking it out to show him.

In the glowing stone, we made out a stretch of brown dusty earth. Crowding around the book, we watched a tiny figure running down a hill, a plume of red dust billowing up behind him.

"It's Max again!" cried Eric. "He's okay. I knew he would be —"

Batamogi gasped. "That red dust means he's in Panjibarrh. He must be nearby!"

As Max ran, we could see a band of Ninns charge over the top of the hill behind him.

"We catch you, furry thing!" cried the

lead Ninn, shaking his fist at Max. All the Ninns' ears were droopy. The warriors were drenched.

"Get over it!" Max yelled. "It was just a boat!"

Then he giggled. "Well, a boat that led a bunch of other boats. All of which are . . . sunk!"

"Way to go, Max," said Neal. "He stopped the Ninns from invading Jaffa City!"

Max scurried to the top of the next hill, slipping and sliding on the dust, then climbed over the ridge. We saw him stop and gasp. "Oh, yes. Ha-ha! Come on, Ninns. Try to follow me — there!"

He ran with all his might to an enormous rock sticking up in the center of the dusty foothills.

Batamogi jumped suddenly. "Bump-alump!"

"Excuse you," said Neal.

"No," he said. "Bumpalump, the big rock that Max is running to. It's been here forever. I can lead you there!"

My heart began to race. "Of course. That's why Thum told us to come here. To find Max!"

"We must get there now," said Ortha.

Batamogi nodded. "Bumpalump is just two hills away. Our dust wheel can take us."

"We'd better hurry," said Eric. "Those Ninns look really mad — as usual!"

As the scene in the Wizardbook stone faded, we ran to the giant wheel in the village center. Everyone crowded around, and we clasped hands as Batamogi and Julie pulled the lever together.

Whrrrr! The giant wheel began to turn faster and faster. A funnel of dust spun up from the ground. It lifted us into the air.

"Here we go again," shouted Neal. "I

hope we don't meet Sparr's car flying around up here —"

Whoo-ooo-osh! The dust storm whirled us around and around, up and over one hill, then another. Finally, we were set down on the very top of the giant rock called Bumpalump.

As the dust storm faded away, we saw that the surface was rough and uneven.

Twee looked around. "Max is not here!"

"But the Ninns are," said Julie, peering down. "They're coming fast. If only we had some banana peels."

"We have something better," I said. "Look!"

Near my feet was a hole in the rock. Below it, a narrow passage carved its way underground.

"I bet that's where Max went," said Eric. "There's something down there. Let's go!"

"Something down there . . ." I whispered.

Seeing my friends jump one by one into the rock, I remembered my mother's words again. Khan, Eric, Ortha, Neal, Woot, Julie, Twee, and Batamogi were with me. So many friends!

But as they slid away inside the rock, I remembered other words.

I was tempted by the darker ways.

I turned and saw the Ninns charge over the top. I watched them slow down when they saw me. I began to speak.

"Kleth . . . nara . . . toom . . ."

They put down their swords and started to bow.

"Nooooo!" I cried as I leaped into the darkness.

Eight

A Face from the Shadows

I shot quickly into a smooth narrow passage.

Everything went dark. The tunnel looped around and up and over, tumbling me down faster and faster. Finally, it leveled out.

Plunk! Oooof! Ayeee! Whoa! Plooop!

I was thrown from the end and landed in a heap. When I stumbled to my feet, I was surprised to find that the floor was flat. "Hello?"

"Everyone's here," Khan said with a cough.

"Except Max," said Batamogi. "He's not here."

"And neither are my sneakers," moaned Neal. "I think I left them about halfway up the passage."

The Ninns were grunting and shouting as they tried to jam themselves into the narrow entrance.

"They'll have a hard time getting down here," said Ortha.

"Somehow, I don't think the Ninns are our biggest worry right now," said Eric. "This Bumpalump is not just any rock. It's sort of . . ."

"Sort of . . . unbelievable!" whispered Julie.

Our eyes had finally gotten used to the

bright light twinkling in from above. And as we looked around, we couldn't believe what we saw.

We were in a room.

High walls. Doorways along one side. A staircase curving down. Tiles on the floor. And in the center of the room, two dark thrones.

"Oh, my gosh —" I whispered.

"Keeah, this is impossible!" said Ortha.

I stared at every part of the room — walls, ceiling, floor, thrones — and I knew.

I had seen this room before.

"It's your parents' throne room in Jaffa City," said Eric. "It's an exact duplicate, except —"

"Except that it's exactly wrong," I said. "Those stairs should be on the wall behind me. At home they lead up, not down. And the thrones —"

The two thrones — the seats of the

king and queen — were made of rough black stone instead of glistening white pearl.

"It's like Jaffa City in reverse," said Khan.

The walls were even draped with banners, but not like the bright silver and green ones at home. Black cloths, tattered, torn, and ragged, waved slowly in the damp air.

"But this isn't possible!" said Batamogi. "Bumpalump has been here forever. How did all this get inside the rock?"

"I think someone is living here," I said, moving ahead. "Let's stay close. With all of us together, maybe we'll be okay. Maybe *I'll* be okay —"

I wanted to tell them about what the Ninns did just before I jumped into the rock.

But the moment I opened my mouth — *vrrrt-vrrrt!* — the floor beneath us began to move. The black tiles shifted, leaving open spaces right under our feet.

"Julie!" said Ortha, trying to pull her away from a moving tile. "Watch out — oh!"

In an instant, the floor opened up under them. When the tiles slid back into place, Julie and Ortha were gone.

Eric jumped. "Where are they? Julie — hey!"

The floor opened up beneath him next. Eric clutched the air wildly, and Batamogi grabbed for him. Together they flew down a tilted shaft.

Fooom! The floor closed back over them.

"Twee!" I shouted. "Woot, look behind you!"

"Help!" the two monkeys screamed together.

They leaped to Khan but all three fell down through the floor in the center of the room. Tiles moved back over them, leaving only Neal and me together on the floor.

"I hear them yelling," said Neal. He stamped on the tiles. "They're down below. Eric! Julie!"

"Stay close," I said. "Give me your hand —"

Wrong move. Neal reached for me, but when he stepped on the tile between us, it slid away and he fell.

"Noooo!" he cried, clutching at the floor.

I jumped to grab him, but he was gone. My Wizardbook went sliding across the stone floor.

"Neal!" I cried. "Neal? Don't leave me here!"

The only sound I heard was a distant *splash*.

I remembered that in Droon, all waters connect. Lakes, pools, rivers, and streams are joined with one another and with the sea.

I also remembered something else my mother had said about her journey.

Finally, I was alone.

I got to my feet. For a second, everything was still, except my heart. It was thundering loudly.

Then — *fwoosh!* — the torches flared up suddenly and gave off a weak orange glow.

"This place does look like Jaffa City," I said. "Just much uglier!"

"What? Don't you like it?" whispered a voice from the shadows. "I call it . . . *Princesstown.*"

So I wasn't alone.

Sparks shot from my hands. "Who's there?"

From the distant corner, lit by a drooping torch's flame, I saw the face of a young girl.

My blood ran cold.

On her head was a crown encircling her long blond hair. When she stepped toward me, I saw that she was dressed in a red tunic and leggings. Around her waist she wore a thick leather belt with a golden buckle.

My mouth opened. "You look like . . ."

"I know," she said. "I look like you. My name is Neffu."

I gasped. "Neffu —"

I remembered the words of my dream.

Krooth-ka . . . meshti . . . pah-la . . . Neffu!

My red sparks sprinkled into the darkness.

"Neffu," I said. The girl looked so much like me. *Too* much like me. "But are you even . . . real?"

"Real enough," she said in a sharp voice. "I am you . . . as a witch."

I felt my knees go weak. Her face was exactly like the one I saw each day in the mirror.

A witch.

"You probably want to know all about me," she said. "I know everything about you."

"No, you don't," I said.

I listened for the sound of my friends. I could barely hear them somewhere in the rock below me. I felt lucky to have so many of them with me. They would help me. They would. If I could find them.

Neffu moved closer, laughing. "Demither gave you dark powers as a child. I know that."

My heart jumped. The girl took another step.

"I was born the day she gave you those

powers," she said. "Right here in this rock. In a little room. I guess you could say those powers *made* me. Over the years, I've been building myself a little palace —"

I looked around. "Playing princess?"

"Practicing my powers," she said sharply.

"I think maybe you've been in this rock a little too long," I said.

She gave a cold laugh. "I agree! Now that your wizard powers have grown, your witch ones have, too. So I'm ready to come out. Actually, I already started. This morning. With you."

My breath caught in my throat. "You made me open the gates for Sparr?"

She smiled.

"You made me turn the guards into toads! You made me steal the Red Eye —"

"Me, me, and, I guess, me!" she said. "I

whispered words to you magically. You heard me."

"The wingwolves," I said. "And the haggons. The Ninns! Every single word that came to me came from you —"

She grinned. "You're welcome! I whispered the old magic of Goll and you used it. There's only one more thing I need to take you over completely."

She reached her hand out to me. It was the color of ice. "Touch me. And I'll be really real!"

"So, you're getting stronger, huh?" I said.

"Every minute!"

Then my wizard powers must be getting stronger, too.

Neffu stood before one of the thrones. "The moment we join hands, I'll take your place. The dark powers will win. Droon

will be mine! You know, all that good stuff. So, come on."

I noticed the Wizardbook on the floor. The stone was glowing. In it, I could see Max again. He was climbing up the wall in a small stone room, trying to escape.

But he wasn't alone.

My heart leaped to see everyone else there, too. Neal, Julie, and Batamogi were with him. Ortha, Twee, Woot, Eric, and Khan, too.

"Oh, yes, your little friends," said Neffu, glancing at the book. "It was nice that Sparr got your parents out of the way. With your friends gone, it will just be us. *Thep-na . . . fo-koosh* —"

As she spoke, the walls rumbled. I could hear Neal and Batamogi call out. The sudden smell of damp air filled my nose. It rose from under the floor. It was the smell of water.

Seawater.

"Say good-bye to your friends," she said.

My hands glowed brighter and brighter. Jagged red sparks scattered and hissed on the floor. "I'll save my friends," I whispered.

"Save yourself instead," she said, holding her hand out to me. *"Poolah . . . no . . . mem —"*

I heard more calls from below.

"Mumble all you want," I said. "You can't tempt me!"

Snatching my Wizardbook, I grabbed a rock from the floor and shot it at the wall next to her.

"What —!" Neffu fired at the noise. *Blam!*

I dived to the stairs and out of the room.

"Get back here!" she cried.

"Yell all you want — I'm outta here!" Feeling my way, I rushed into the passages ahead — down, down, down. The stones were damp and slippery beneath my feet.

But I knew where I was going.

If Neffu's palace was the opposite of Jaffa City, her room — *my room!* — wouldn't be at the top of the palace. It would be buried at the bottom.

It would be like a dungeon!

Neffu said that's where she was born.

That's where it all began.

And that's where it would have to end.

One more hallway, then quickly down the wet steps to her room. I rushed through the door and stopped.

My heart swelled. The floor of the room was a pool as dark as the walls. It smelled of the ocean.

I hoped the waters in this dark palace

connected with all the others in Droon. I spoke the name of the only one who could help me.

One second . . . two seconds . . .

The surface of the pool splashed and a mass of green hair rose from the water.

A face appeared from the depths of the pool.

She had answered my call.

"Demither!"

Nine

Royal Family

The serpent witch arched up to the ceiling of the small room.

Her tail slapped up from the pool, swished through the air once, then slithered under the water again.

"Keeah," said Demither.

Her voice echoed sharply against the stones. Her lips were black, her skin paler than ever.

I was afraid of her, but I knew I had to speak.

"Long ago," I said, "you shared your dark powers with me. Why?"

She stared at me with deep eyes. "To fight Sparr. You needed them then —"

"Those powers are taking over now."

The Sea Witch nodded. "I did not know it, but Neffu was born that day. As your wizard magic has grown, the dark magic I gave you has also. And with it, *she* has grown. While you slept, she told you words, charms, spells. . . ."

"She made me let Sparr into our city!" I said.

The witch's head moved from side to side like a snake watching me. "Neffu wants to take you over. Then you'll truly be a witch, as Sparr wants."

"I won't let it happen to me," I said.

"You won't let it?" cried Demither. "I was a wizard like your mother — it happened to me!"

Her shiny skin flashed in the light, making the room glow green.

It was then that I saw a black medal nearly hidden by the scales on her neck.

Carved deeply on the medal was a shape I knew. A triangle pointing down, sharp horns curving up from the upper angles, and a lightning bolt driving straight down the middle.

It was an ancient symbol, from the earliest language of Droon.

It was a name.

Sparr.

Demither twisted and writhed in the pool, knowing I had seen the amulet. "It would take more power than you have to remove this curse!" she said. "I am Sparr's servant. I turned away from my family, from you, from everything —"

Booom-ooom! Neffu was blasting in the halls, yelling, coming closer.

"Keeah, listen!" said Demither, her eyes flashing. "I answered your call for a reason. One day, sorcerers and wizards will meet in a great struggle."

I shuddered. "I hoped it would never happen —"

"It will. And when that day comes, Sparr will call on me, even against my will, to help him."

My heart pounded. I couldn't take my eyes off the black medal.

Demither's eyes grew large. A red glow seemed to burst from them, then she looked away. "Do not let Neffu win! One becomes a *droomar*, but one chooses to be a witch. The dark powers are strong, but remember — until she becomes real, Neffu is magic, just magic. Nothing more!"

With that, she dived under the surface of the pool.

"Demither, wait!" I shouted.

Her tail slid away under the water.

I stared at the pool. She was gone.

"Demither," I whispered, "if I ever get the chance, I will set you free!"

Suddenly, the room lit up with a red glow.

Neffu ran in, breathing hard. "So, you found my little room. Not bad, huh? But I think I'm ready for a change. A new room in Jaffa City. In the palace. Like your room, perhaps?"

But I had already decided.

"Sorry, Neffy," I said. "I think living here has made you a bit wacky. Dark powers and all."

"Dark powers?" she said. "Do you want to see what dark powers can do? Take a look!"

She murmured under her breath, "*Pleth-ku . . . mala . . . tengo . . . hoo . . .*"

All of a sudden, the damp air swirled with moving shapes. I saw wheels creaking and thousands of pilka hooves thundering toward us from a hazy distance.

"Is this some kind of vision?" I asked.

"I want you to see what could be ours!"

Then came chariots. I saw dozens of green groggles harnessed to golden cars, Ninn warriors inside, grunting and cheering. They raced right through the room and vanished.

Next came rivers of gold. They seemed to flow around the room's dark walls, then fade away.

"All this will be ours for the asking!" she said.

A sudden blare of trumpets sounded, and I saw myself enthroned in the court-yard of Jaffa City, surrounded by Ninns blurting out a song.

Keeah here! Keeah there!
She's our princess everywhere!

Neffu laughed. "You like?" She laughed again, and her face became as hard and cruel as Sparr's face. And from behind her ears, beginning to sprout and grow, came burning red fins.

"It's time!" she snarled. "Any last words?"

That's when it came to me.

Words.

Galen always says power comes from words.

I closed my eyes, and words filled my head, thousands of them. But of all of them, one word sounded the loudest.

From the moment I heard it, I knew it was a word of great magic and power. But it wasn't strange-sounding or from an ancient language.

It was a common word.

An everyday word.

A word I heard all the time.

And in my mind, I heard only one voice speaking it. My own.

I breathed in and opened my eyes.

All of a sudden, the dark room seemed to go still. And for an instant, I saw . . . *everything.*

The sights and sounds of Neffu's magic visions were gone. Flooding my ears instead was the murmur of a million voices.

And a million hearts beating all over Droon.

On the wall in front of me, I saw a bead of water trickle down the stones as if it were a diamond, leaving a thin silver trail behind it.

I heard the whisper of the tattered black banners above and of the green and silver cloths hanging at home in Jaffa City.

The air itself seemed not dim and damp but tingling and alive with thousands of points of sparkling light.

It was beautiful!

And I knew what it was.

The Elfin Sight!

That's when I knew I could defeat Neffu.

"So, are you ready?" she asked coldly.

I looked at the witch. "In a second," I said.

Then I leaned over the pool and twisted my belt in the reflection, first one way, then another.

"There. Perfect."

"What was that all about?" Neffu asked.

"My father always says you should straighten your tunic before battle."

"Battle?" Her face turned hard. The fins behind her ears turned black. "So, you're not joining me?"

"It's the red tunic," I said. "It's not really my color."

BLAMMM! I sent a blast at her feet — a bright blue blast of wizard sparks. It sent her back to the wall.

"I'll get you —" she howled. "You — *you!*"

"Now you sound like a Ninn!" I snapped. "No offense to the Ninns! Oh, and since you like words so much — *snippity-ippity-plum-jumm!*"

Instantly, the vision of a chariot roared into the room. Ninns urged the groggles to go faster.

"You're nothing but magic?" I said. "Well, here's your magic ride!"

With one more blast — *whoom!* — I sent her into the passing chariot. "Bye now!"

"I'll come back!" she screamed. "I'll barge into that pink room of yours and I'll — ohhhh!"

Just before she went speeding away, I yanked the gold crown from her head. An instant later, the chariot drove straight through the ceiling and was gone. When the vision faded, the crown fell through my fingers, nothing more than dust.

"I figured," I said. "Just magic."

The rock rumbled again.

I dashed back into the hall and shot up the stairs. "Eric! Max! Ortha! Julie!"

My friends shouted back from somewhere above me. More stairs, more halls. The rock began to crumble. "I'm coming!"

"Keeah —" called Eric.

BLAMMM! I blasted the wall in front of me.

All my friends came tumbling out. And from across the room, a furry little shape ran to me.

Max leaped into my arms. "Oh, my princess!"

I hugged him tight. "Max! I'm so sorry for blasting you out to sea!"

"But no!" he chirped. "You sent me away from Jaffa City for a reason. If you hadn't, I never would have been able to scuttle the Ninn boats. They never would have chased me here. It all led me back to you! Now *that* is true wizardry!"

Boom! Krrrackkkk! Thunnnk! The giant rock quaked all around us.

"With Neffu gone," I said, "her palace is crumbling."

"We'd better get out of here!" said Neal.

The ceiling began to fall in giant chunks.

"Booby trap!" yelled Julie.

"Bumpalump booby trap!" shouted Batamogi.

Ten

The Nose Knows

Huge pieces of ceiling shattered on every side. Neffu's home was crumbling around us. The Bumpalump was cracking apart.

"The ugly palace is coming down!" cried Twee. "We'll be squished!"

Whammm! A wall tumbled down at our feet.

Suddenly, Julie pointed to a hole breaking open in the floor. "Daylight. A way out —"

We rushed toward the light, but two walls were sliding together in front of it.

"We won't make it!" cried Batamogi.

"I can!" said Neal. He ran, then dropped to the floor, his wet clothes helping him slide between the closing walls. He stopped in the gap and jammed a stone between the walls.

"I hate being wet," he crowed, "but the slippery thing works for me! Everyone out of here — fast!"

We jumped between the walls and down through the floor, where we found another rock slide. Daylight glinted below.

"Here we go again!" I cried.

Whooosh! Down and around and up and down we flew. In passage after passage, we twisted and tumbled, thrown together and split apart.

"Wheeee!" Khan shouted, bumping Twee into Woot and Max into Batamogi.

Finally — *whoomp! whoomp!* — we flew out of the stone and tumbled away from the quaking Bumpalump.

A gang of Ninns were also running away from the crumbling rock. "Get away!" they yelled. "Keeah not lead us!"

We rolled to safety while more and more rocks tumbled down around us. After what seemed like a long time, the quaking stopped. The dust cleared.

And we stared.

"Oh, my goodness," Ortha whispered.

Julie gasped. "Um . . . whoa."

"Pretty much me, too," said Eric.

Batamogi gulped. "The Bumpalump — is not the Bumpalump!"

The enormous stone was no longer a mass of jagged rock. It was now a giant head, looking east toward the Dark Lands.

"It's like what Thum told us," said Eric.

"Droon's future lies in the one with the biggest head."

"And that's the biggest head ever," said Julie. "Keeah, it's you. The face is you!"

It was me. My face. My eyes. My hair and crown.

And no fins growing behind the ears.

My heart soared to see the stone sculpture.

"It's a sign," said Ortha.

"A sign?" said Neal, looking up at the head. "It's nice and everything, but I think we just fell out of the nose!"

Plop-plop! Neal's two sneakers came down from the nose and struck him on the head.

"Things are looking up," he mumbled.

"Speaking of looking up," gasped Batamogi. "Look there — haggons!"

We turned to see the three hag sisters

circling overhead. *"Keeeeeeaahhh!"* they shrieked.

I raised my hands in the air. Blue sparks sprinkled from them.

"Attack-k-k-k-k!" the haggons howled.

"Guys," I said, "I think they figured out I'm not their leader anymore. This time they *will* attack."

"But maybe we can choose the place," said Batamogi. He turned to Julie. "Can you take us back to our village right now?"

Julie's eyes sparkled. "I think I can!" she said. "Everybody grab hold of one another. Keeah, Ortha, you take my hands. Here we *gooooo!*"

We held hands tightly — all ten of us — and Julie lifted into the air. Together we flew up and soared back to the village.

The haggons flapped noisily behind us, shrieking and snarling at my bright blue sparks.

"So," the first one said, grinding her two teeth together. "Keeah is our enemy again?"

"She always was a goody-goody," snarled the second. "And we are the baddy-baddies!"

"Plus, I never did like *blue*!" the third one howled. "Are you ready to attack, sisters?"

They began to circle the little village.

"Should we use our magic?" asked Eric.

"Maybe there's a better idea." I looked over at the dust wheel. "Batamogi?"

"Just what I was thinking," he said. "Oobja!"

"Dive, sisters — dive," shrieked the haggons.

Batamogi and everyone from the village raced to the big wooden wheel in the square.

"Now!" he said. They pulled the lever hard.

Whrr-whrr-whrr! The wheel turned faster and faster, and more and more dust whirled around until — *whoosh!* — a funnel shot up at the haggons.

Dust spun in their faces, and they sneezed — *aaaa-chooo!* — over and over again. The force of the sneezes threw them to the ground. They sat up sneezing even more.

Finally, the largest one grunted. "This is just too hard. Come, sisters. Let's go back to the Dark Lands. Sparr is on his own!"

The three hag dragons flew up over the dust hills, sneezed some more, and were gone.

"May Droon be with you!" I called.

The Oobja cheered loudly. And my friends joined in, too.

I looked around. Everyone was with me. Three friends from the Upper World.

Three from the Bangledorn Forest. My trusted spider troll friend. The leader of the Lumpies. The Oobja king and all his people.

My heart lifted as if it had wings.

"To Jaffa City!" I cried.

Using my mother's words again, I waved my hands, and together we flew back across Droon in a tube of spinning blue light.

We raced over the ground, passing the great Rivertangle, the deserts of Lumpland, the giant Bangledorn Forest.

"My beautiful Droon is almost safe," I whispered.

"Thanks to you," said Eric, smiling.

But I knew that the most dangerous part of the journey was still to come.

We would have to face Lord Sparr himself.

By the time we got in sight of the city

walls, there were only a few minutes left before the halting spell ended. Soon the city would be alive again.

Whoosh! We soared over the palace and into the courtyard. It had been nearly twelve hours since that morning. Already, the sun was setting over the western sea. The ocean's dark waves flashed gold in the last of the light.

"It's nearly time," said Julie.

We charged into the palace together.

We raced right to the throne room.

I stopped. My parents were still trapped in their crystal box, their eyes closed in sleep.

"Soon," I said.

In the center of the room, Sparr stood silent, a gloating smile fixed on his face.

"Children, hide behind the banner," said Max. "I'll climb to the rafters. Khan, would you care to come?"

"And us, too!" said Twee.

"Certainly," said the Lumpy king.

All together, Khan, Max, and the three Bangledorn monkeys climbed to the ceiling.

I took my place, stepping up to Lord Sparr.

As he moved behind the curtain with Neal, Julie, and Batamogi, Eric turned to me. "This is your moment, Keeah. Good luck."

I smiled. "Thanks."

The room went silent.

Three seconds . . . two seconds . . .

Then I heard the soft scratch of the sorcerer's cloak moving over the stones.

It was time.

Eleven

Just Magic

Whooosh! The spell ended. Everything came alive at once.

My heart trembled as I saw Sparr move.

He noticed me instantly, narrowing his gaze. "You stopped everything."

Closing my eyes for a moment, I sensed Max and Ortha scampering across the ceiling, as stealthy as mice.

I heard my father's slow breathing in

the crystal box, my mother's heart beating in her sleep. I felt Eric, Julie, and Neal waiting behind the curtain.

It was the Elfin Sight.

I saw and heard everything.

I opened my eyes. "I needed time to think."

"And?" said Sparr.

"I've made my choice," I said.

Sparr stepped forward. "And?"

I smiled. "Show me the power we'll use to rule. Show me . . . the Red Eye of Dawn!"

Keeah — Eric said silently.

Wait . . . I answered, also silently. I told him we needed to use our powers at just the right moment.

Okay, said Eric.

The sorcerer paused, his eyes glinting. Then he grinned. "Why not? Look there. The day is nearly over. The sun is almost under the horizon. Time for sleep? But no! See what the Red Eye can do. See what power is ours!"

He stepped to the doorway and out onto the balcony, overlooking the vast ocean of Droon. He opened his hand.

WHOOOOM! A blast of red lightning exploded from the crimson jewel.

It shot across the waves. It struck the sun.

Then, as Sparr slowly drew the jewel up in the air, the sun itself rose back up, inch by inch, until streaks of pink light slanted over the balcony stones.

Staring at the rising sun, I remembered what my father had said last night.

The day Demither turned away from her family was the day she lost her Elfin Sight.

I vowed that would never happen to me. But I also knew that Demither was my mother's sister. She was my family. We were bound together. I knew it in Neffu's room when, above all the others, I heard that one word.

The word of greatest magic.

Love.

Closing my eyes, I used my Elfin Sight to search the watery passages under our world.

I found her.

Demither! I called across the miles.

When I opened my eyes — *splash!* — the waves broke open and her giant serpent's form burst up, coiling and twisting in the air.

Sparr, still holding the jewel aloft, laughed suddenly. "Demither? Of course. Keeah, Demither, and me. The three dark powers of Droon are all here as we take over. How *perfect!*"

I shuddered to hear the word.

Demither had to be free of Sparr, if only so she could choose for herself. *That* would be perfect.

"You like?" asked Sparr, drawing the sun higher, casting its glow over the white floor tiles.

My fingers heated up. I looked down. A blue beam of light shot from my hands. As I watched, the sparks turned red, and finally violet.

It was time. I turned to the curtains.

One . . . two . . . three . . .

Blammm! I blasted the crystal box. It shattered into a thousand shards of glass and blue sparks. My parents opened their eyes and rushed out.

"Mother!" I shouted. "Get ready —"

"What?" cried Sparr, turning.

"I'll tell you *what*," said Eric, bursting from the curtain. "You're on our turf now, Sparr!"

Everyone jumped out from behind the curtain. Max and the others leaped from the ceiling.

Sparr's fins flashed a burning red. "What's all this?"

"Keeah has a big family!" said Julie.

"Now!" I shouted. "A single beam of light!"

My mother and Eric turned to the sea. We shot beams out over the water.

Violet. Blue. Silver. Our blasts joined.

"What?" cried Sparr. "No —"

KKKKK! The sky lit up with a brilliant, many-colored blast. It met the ray from the Red Eye and turned it away from the sun.

And right onto Demither. The blast struck her with a bright flash. Shrieking, she rose like a monster over the bay.

"No! No!" howled Sparr, closing his fist. But by the time the light went dim, it was too late.

Something tiny whizzed through the air.

Plink! A small black medal dropped to the stones at Sparr's feet. He picked it up.

I laughed. "Your amulet fell off, Sparr. You don't have Demither's power. She isn't your servant anymore. She's . . . free!"

Demither stared at me with her yellow eyes. She dived and burst up near the city walls, arching high over all of us. Then, flipping her tail hard, she sent a spray of seawater over Sparr.

She drenched him completely.

"Hey, I know what that's like!" said Neal.

An instant later, she was gone.

Max jumped. "Look at that! I know *them!*"

A tiny rowboat swayed into the harbor. A handful of Ninns stumbled toward the palace. They waved at Sparr.

The sorcerer's fins turned black and rimmed with fire. He stared at me.

"KEEAH, YOU SHALL PAY FOR THIS!"

Everyone rushed to my side. Eric and my mother had their hands ready. My father wielded a giant wooden club. Julie, Ortha, and the others were ready to charge. Neal even had a bucket of water ready to throw.

"This just isn't your day," said Julie.

"Call it quits," added Eric.

Quivering, Sparr raised his hands to me. "Why — you!" He sent a blast at me.

Don't fire! I said. *I have a better idea.*

Even as his bolt came at me, I jumped at him.

I spun around in the air, not touching down. It was as if everything slowed while I alone moved. I dodged his lightning bolt, then everything sped up again.

My foot met his shoulder.

Whump! He was pushed back ten feet. His shot went wild, and he teetered on the edge of the balcony.

"Sorry, Sparr," I said, coming down. "These new wizard powers are *soooo* tricky!"

He swayed back, then finally fell from the balcony. "Ninns!" he cried out. "Catch me —"

We ran to the edge.

The red warriors hustled across the grass, holding out their hands for him. Then they suddenly jerked back, as if afraid of being hurt.

"What — no —" Sparr cried out.

Blumffff! He thudded to the ground.

He lay there on the grass, his dark eyes rolling in his head.

Finally, he wobbled to his feet. "I still have the Red Eye of Dawn! You will see its great power — *my* great power — as you never have before. The Empire of Shadows begins now!"

As I watched Sparr limp to the sea, his hands clasped over the red jewel, I realized something.

The great magical *things* he might discover or create didn't seem to matter so much.

They were . . . just magic.

"Take the Eye," I said. "The Golden Wasp, the Coiled Viper. Take them all. Together, we're more than a match for you."

Right at that exact moment — *kawhoooom!* — something large and heavy crashed to the earth in a crumpled heap next to Sparr. He gasped, his mouth hanging open.

"Oh, my gosh," said Batamogi. "So that's where that went. It traveled a long way!"

It was Sparr's yellow car.

It had finally come down.

Completely smashed.

"Oh, yeah," said Eric. "We borrowed the car. It got pretty wrecked, though. Sorry."

My father boomed a loud laugh. "Can we offer you a ride home?"

Saying nothing, Sparr turned away. His Ninns crowded around and helped him into what was left of their great fleet of ships. We watched as the little rowboat splashed away from the city and was gone.

"Yahoo!" cried Neal.

"Yay, Keeah!" shouted Julie.

Eric smiled. "We won today."

"Keeah!" my father boomed, rushing to me and swinging me around.

My mother kissed me, then looked into my eyes. "The Elfin Sight. You have it —"

"And not a minute too soon!" I said.

Surrounding me were Ortha, Woot,

Twee, Batamogi, Khan, Max, Eric, Julie, Neal, and my parents.

My family.

After all that had happened, it was amazing to have them all here for this moment.

It was perfect.

"The *droomar* would be so proud of you today," said my mother.

"Oh, we are!" said a familiar voice.

Twelve

The Soul's Language

I turned and saw the old brown hat hovering on the balcony. The little elf appeared below it.

"Thum!" I said, running to him. "I'm glad you remembered to come!"

"I almost didn't," he said as he drifted across the stones to us. My mother hugged him.

"You really helped us today," said Julie.

"You helped Keeah most of all," said my mother. "Thank you!"

The little creature bowed. "Ooooo, yes. But really Keeah helped us. She was inspired by what she saw in the stone of her Wizardbook."

I held the book close to me. It seemed to call out to me to begin writing in it.

"Bring the tea," my father boomed. "This calls for a great feast. Keeah is a *droomar* today!"

Almost instantly, dozens of kitchen workers brought out pot after pot of Droon tea and huge platters of food to go with it.

"Talk about magic," said Neal, "it's like they can read my mind."

"Talk about magic," I said, "look at this." I sprayed a narrow stream of blue sparks from my right hand and red ones from my left.

"That is so cool," said Eric. "When did you learn you could do that?"

"In Neffu's palace," I said. "The Elfin Sight showed me how even the dark powers can be used for good! Look at this, too."

I lightly touched the tips of my thumbs together and sprayed out a glowing stream of blue and red sparks together.

"Violet sparks," gasped Julie. "So awesome!"

But the most awesome part was how all my friends stayed to party with me for hours.

Lights went on all over the city. People began dancing through the streets. The great palace fountain bubbled softly with the fresh, sweet water of summer.

When twilight came, my father stood over the courtyard and yelled.

"To the newest *droomar* wizard!"

"*O — lee — lee!*" yelled Ortha, Twee, and Woot together.

A great cheer went up all over town. The guards, not toads anymore, waved the bright green and silver banners high.

Finally, my father unscrewed the horns from his helmet and blew a big blast of air through both of them. *Woooo-hoooo!*

They made the sweetest music.

Until the moon came up, my mother sang harp songs and Max danced. His eight legs flew around as if there were two of him!

All evening, we knew Droon was safe.

Neal chuckled. "Sparr is too tired to try anything now."

Finally — *whoosh!* — the rainbow staircase appeared over the courtyard.

As my friends stepped onto the glistening steps, Eric paused and turned.

"We went a long way today," he said.

"We saw a lot of stuff," said Neal. "And found out a lot of things."

"We did," I said.

"But some things we knew all along," said Julie, giving me a hug.

Eric laughed. "You took the words right out of my mouth. Keeah, you'll always be a wizard to us. And we'll be back before you know it."

"Yeah," said Neal. "I have a feeling there are a lot of things to get done!"

Laughing, my three friends ran up the staircase and away into the clouds.

I closed my eyes and heard a faint squeak, then a click, as the door at the top of the stairs closed. Then the stairs faded.

"See you soon," I whispered.

Five minutes later, I was sitting cross-legged under the stars on the little balcony outside my room.

I could just hear the sounds of my father singing and my mother's bright laughter as they made their way through the halls of the palace below.

I had more power than ever before. With my mother's help, I would learn to use every bit of it to make sure Droon was always safe.

And when Galen came back — and I knew he would return to us soon — there would be nothing we couldn't do together.

Besides, everywhere I looked, I found people who loved me. People who I loved.

I remembered that simple word again.

Love.

"*Snkk-grrr-snkk!* Yes, yes! In a moment!"

I turned to see Max curled up like a ball of fur, muttering and snoring in his little bed.

Yes, everywhere I looked there was love.

I pointed a finger to the small rose-colored candle on my nightstand and whispered words Galen had taught me.

"*Sepp-o-bah . . .*"

Fwishh! The candle stand wobbled, then whisked itself up off the table. It set itself down with a soft *plonk* on the tiles in front of me.

I winked, and the candle flared into life.

Moving the Wizardbook to my lap, I looked at the stone on its cover.

This time, it showed nothing but my own face.

I opened the book to where the very first page gazed up at me, blank, white, clean, and ready.

Looking up, I saw that the moon was full.

In its glow, the sky was wide and blue and streaked with violet.

Violet. The color of my powers.

So.

Midnight.

The candle flickered its warm flame over the blank page. I thought of the wonderful, magical words I would write.

I looked around and listened to the quiet sounds of Droon at night.

Everything was perfect.

Dipping my pen in ink, I set it on the page, breathed once, and began to write.

It was the sound of words that woke me. . . .

About the Author

Tony Abbott is the author of more than fifty funny novels for young readers, including the popular *Danger Guys* books and *The Weird Zone* series. Since childhood he has been drawn to stories that challenge the imagination, and, like Eric, Julie, and Neal, he often dreamed of finding doors that open to other worlds. Now that he is older — though not quite as old as Galen Longbeard — he believes he may have found some of those doors. They are called books. Tony Abbott was born in Ohio and now lives with his wife and two daughters in Connecticut.

For more information about Tony Abbott and the continuing saga of Droon, visit www.tonyabbottbooks.com.

THE SECRETS OF DROON

by
by Tony Abbott

Under the stairs, a magical world awaits you!

- ❏ BDK 0-590-10839-5   #1: The Hidden Stairs and the Magic Carpet
- ❏ BDK 0-590-10841-7   #2: Journey to the Volcano Palace
- ❏ BDK 0-590-10840-9   #3: The Mysterious Island
- ❏ BDK 0-590-10842-5   #4: City in the Clouds
- ❏ BDK 0-590-10843-3   #5: The Great Ice Battle
- ❏ BDK 0-590-10844-1   #6: The Sleeping Giant of Goll
- ❏ BDK 0-439-18297-2   #7: Into the Land of the Lost
- ❏ BDK 0-439-18298-0   #8: The Golden Wasp
- ❏ BDK 0-439-20772-X   #9: The Tower of the Elf King
- ❏ BDK 0-439-20784-3   #10: Quest for the Queen
- ❏ BDK 0-439-20785-1   #11: The Hawk Bandits of Tarkoom
- ❏ BDK 0-439-20786-X   #12: Under the Serpent Sea
- ❏ BDK 0-439-30606-X   #13: The Mask of Maliban
- ❏ BDK 0-439-30607-8   #14: Voyage of the *Jaffa Wind*
- ❏ BDK 0-439-30608-6   #15: The Moon Scroll
- ❏ BDK 0-439-30609-4   #16: The Knights of Silversnow
- ❏ BDK 0-439-42078-4   #17: Dream Thief
- ❏ BDK 0-439-42079-2   #18: Search for the Dragon Ship
- ❏ BDK 0-439-42080-6   #19: The Coiled Viper
- ❏ BDK 0-439-56040-3   #20: In the Ice Caves of Krog
- ❏ BDK 0-439-56043-8   #21: Flight of the Genie

$3.99 each!

- ❏ BDK 0-439-42077-6   Special Edition #1: The Magic Escapes $4.99

Available Wherever You Buy Books or Use This Order Form

www.scholastic.com

■ SCHOLASTIC

SODBL100

MEET
Geronimo Stilton

A REPORTER WITH A NOSE FOR GREAT STORIES

Who is Geronimo Stilton? Why, that's me! I run a newspaper, but my true passion is writing tales of adventure. Here on Mouse Island, my books are all bestsellers! What's that? You've never read one? Well, my books are full of fun. They are whisker-licking-good stories, and that's a promise!

www.scholastic.com/kids

■SCHOLASTIC

GERSTT

MORE SERIES YOU'LL LOVE

For fun, magic, and mystery, say...

Abracadabra!

The members of the Abracadabra Club
have a few tricks up their sleeves—
and a few tricks you can
learn to do yourself!

™ Jigsaw and his partner, Mila,
know that mysteries are like
jigsaw puzzles—you've got to look
at all the pieces to solve the case!

Hey L'il D!

L'il Dobber has two things
with him at all times—his
basketball and his friends.
Together, they are a great team. And they
are always looking for adventure and fun—
on and off the b'ball court!